THE ALEPH-BET STORY BOOK

THE
ALEPH-BET
STORY BOOK

By DEBORAH PESSIN

Drawings by Howard Simon

PHILADELPHIA
THE JEWISH PUBLICATION SOCIETY OF AMERICA

60

PRINTED IN THE UNITED STATES OF AMERICA

To
David

Acknowledgments

I wish to express my gratitude to Dr. Azriel Eisenberg, who suggested a book of alphabet stories; to Dr. Solomon Grayzel and Maurice Jacobs, of The Jewish Publication Society of America, whose encouragement made the work possible; and to my husband — fellow fantasizer.

TABLE OF CONTENTS

THE ALEPH-BET STORY BOOK

Aleph Introduces the Alphabet

IT WAS in the early days of the world. Everything was new. The leaves of the trees sparkled with dew. The grass was crisp and green. Birds that had just been born were singing their first songs. All the world was bright and gay.

In the Garden of Eden, which was the first garden in the world, there was a new man. His name was Adam.

Adam was very busy in the Garden of Eden learning about everything. He examined all the flowers and the trees. He watched the tiny insects as they crawled along the ground. He walked up the hills to see what was on the other side, and he followed the river current to see where it would lead.

The animals showed him their dens in the forests of the Garden of Eden. The buzzing insects that flew from flower to flower showed him how honey was made.

The animals that lived in the branches of the trees taught Adam how to climb trees. And the fish taught him how to swim in the cool river.

At night, when Adam lay on his bed of pine needles, he watched the moon sail overhead. Sometimes he watched the bright glittering stars till they faded and dawn came over the rim of the hills.

Adam was happy in the Garden of Eden. The birds and the animals were his friends. When he was hungry, he ate the fruit of the trees. When he was thirsty, he drank the water of the brooks and the springs.

At last, when Adam had learned all about

the Garden of Eden, he decided that it was time to give everything a name. But he needed an alphabet for making up names.

Now it just happened that when Adam decided he needed an alphabet, the Hebrew alphabet was on its way to visit him. There were twenty-two letters in the Hebrew alphabet, and they were all very eager to meet the first man, Adam.

When they came to the Garden of Eden, they walked through the gate, one by one. Aleph, who was the first letter of the alphabet, went first. The rest followed in alphabetical order.

"Good morning, Adam," said Aleph.

"Good morning," said Adam as he looked at Aleph curiously. "Who are you? There is nothing like you in the Garden of Eden."

"I am Aleph," said Aleph, "the first letter of the Hebrew alphabet."

"And I am the first man," said Adam, "so we ought to be good friends."

Then Aleph introduced all the other letters. And Adam was very happy to know the Hebrew alphabet. For now he was ready to give everything in the Garden of Eden a name.

Bet
and the
Bashful Animal

IT WAS time for Adam to give names to the animals in the Garden of Eden. Adam asked the letters of the Hebrew alphabet to help him.

He cupped his hands around his mouth and let his voice ring through the Garden of Eden. The animals came running from far and near. They crowded around Adam and waited for their names.

It took a long time because there were so many of them. And they were hard to please. The big animals wanted big names and the small animals wanted small names. Some of the big animals wanted small names and some of the small animals wanted big names. And all the special animals wanted special names — like the one with a pouch to carry her young ones.

Some animals were never satisfied. When Adam gave the donkey his name he became very stubborn. No matter what name Adam suggested, he objected. He wanted something better. At last Adam told him not to be mulish. He would have to take the name he had suggested at first.

Finally all the animals had names. They went off to their lairs and dens. Adam rubbed his hands together and a pleased look came over his face. But a moment later the pleased look disappeared.

"One animal is missing," he said.

"Who?" asked the letters of the alphabet.

"I don't know," said Adam. "I mean," he went on in a confused sort of way, "I

7

don't know his name because he doesn't have one."

"What is he like?" the letters asked.

"He's very bashful," said Adam. "Maybe that's why he didn't come. He must be hiding somewhere."

"Don't worry, Adam," said the letters, "we'll find him."

"Whoever finds him," Adam promised, "will be the first letter of his name."

The letters scampered off to find the Bashful Animal. They looked here and they looked there. They looked in tree tops and behind stones. They looked everywhere.

The letter Bet, which is the second letter of the Hebrew alphabet, went off by himself to the north of the Garden of Eden.

He wandered through fields. He walked through a forest where he almost lost his way. He searched under boulders and among the tall grass of the pastures.

At last Bet came to a hill. When he reached the top of the hill he was so tired that he sat down to rest. Suddenly the hill began to move.

Bet was frightened.

"Help!" he shouted. "Help!"

The hill stopped moving. Bet looked around. It was a very smooth hill he was standing on, without grass or shrubs or trees anywhere.

"Strange," thought Bet. "I never saw a hill like this before."

And he began to climb down again.

Once more the hill moved. Bet stood very still, too frightened to take another step. Then he heard a loud voice say, "Whoever you are, please get off my back."

The voice seemed to come from the front of the hill. Bet began to move forward to see who was talking. The hill squirmed and shook from top to bottom. Then the loud voice said again, "I wish you wouldn't do that. I'm sure you wouldn't like things moving around on *your* back."

"Oh," said Bet, "then it's the hill that's talking."

"I'm not a hill," said the voice. "I'm an animal."

Bet was so surprised he almost went tumbling to the ground.

"You must be the Bashful Animal," he said. "We've been looking for you everywhere. Why didn't you come for your name?"

"Because everyone stares at me," said the Bashful Animal. "I can't help it if I'm as big as a hill."

"Please come back with me," said Bet. "Adam is very unhappy because you haven't a name."

"I don't want a name," said the Bashful Animal. "I just want them to stop looking at me all the time."

"But all the animals have names," Bet said. "You don't want everyone to keep calling you Bashful Animal."

Bet coaxed and pleaded. But the Bashful Animal refused to budge.

"It doesn't have to be a special kind of name," said Bet. "Just a name. And I'll be the first letter."

"Well, all right," said the Bashful Animal at last. "But please tell the others to stop staring at me all the time."

And he began to move with seven-league strides through the Garden of Eden. Bet rode high on his back, his head almost reaching the sky. They crossed fields and hills and valleys, and soon they came to the part of the Garden of Eden where Adam lived.

All the other letters had given up the search long ago. They were wondering what could have happened to Bet, when he came riding along on the animal which was as big as a hill.

Everyone was glad to see them. The animals gathered about and began to stare.

"You see," the Bashful Animal said to Bet, "I told you."

"Please don't stare at him like that," said Bet. "It isn't his fault if he's so big."

"I want a simple name," the Bashful Animal told Adam. "Nothing too special."

"And don't forget to put me at the beginning," said Bet.

Adam thought and thought. All the letters thought. The Bashful Animal looked at them hopefully.

Finally Adam thought of a name.

"I know," he said. "We'll call you Behemoth. That's a nice, modest name which means Animal. It's just right for your bashful nature."

Behemoth was satisfied with his modest name.

"Now I am just an animal like all the others," he said. "Perhaps they will stop staring at me."

The Friendship of Gimel and Gamal

THE letter Gimel had a friend in the Garden of Eden. His name was Gamal, which means camel. Gimel and Gamal resembled each other. They both had long necks and their names were almost the same.

Every day Gimel went to visit Gamal the Camel. He liked to sit on his friend's back and ride around in the Garden of Eden. He even tried to imitate his camel friend. Gimel would practice walking with swaying motions.

And he pretended he had humps on his back.

After a while the animals in the Garden of Eden began to wonder who was Gimel and who was Gamal.

Now the letters of the Hebrew alphabet did not like Gimel's running off every day to see Gamal the Camel. It was a nuisance, they said. When they were making up words and needed Gimel, they had to go looking for him.

The letters decided to see Gamal the Camel. They thought that perhaps he could help.

"A letter's place is in the alphabet," they told Gamal, "not between the humps of a camel."

Gamal the Camel pushed his lips in and out as he thought it over. Then he said to Gimel, "You had better go along with the rest of the alphabet. I'll come to visit you every day."

Gimel returned to the alphabet. The next day Gamal the Camel came to visit him. He squatted beside Gimel and watched the letters as they made up words.

The next day Gamal came again.

And the next day.

And the next.

He came every day and squatted beside Gimel as he sat in his place in the alphabet.

Soon Gamal began to imitate Gimel. He tried to help make up words, too. Whenever the letters needed Gimel for a word, Gamal said, "How about me? Won't I do?" Gimel, who was his friend, said, "Of course. Why not?" But the other letters, who were more sensible, said, "Certainly not. Gamal is a camel and Gimel is a letter and you can't use Gamal when a word needs Gimel."

One day Gamal got the letters all mixed up. He pleaded so much to get into a word that they made a mistake and put him in instead of Gimel. That spoiled the word,

of course, and they had to begin all over again.

The letters were annoyed. They asked Gamal to stop visiting Gimel so often. His place, they said, was with the animals, not in the alphabet.

Gamal the Camel sadly pushed his lips in and out. He looked as though he were going to cry. The letters did not know what to do. They decided to see Adam and tell him about it. They went off, leaving Gamal and Gimel together.

Soon they returned with Adam.

"So there you are," said Adam when he saw Gamal. "I've been wondering what happened to you."

"I want to remain with the alphabet," Gamal explained.

"But the animals need a camel," said Adam. "They can't get along without you."

Gamal was glad to hear that the animals could not get along without him. He got to his feet.

Gimel got to his feet, too.

"And the alphabet needs a Gimel," said Adam. "They can't get along without a Gimel."

Gimel was glad to hear that the letters could not get along without him. He sat down again.

"Good-by, Gimel," said Gamal.

"Good-by, Gamal," said Gimel.

And Gamal went off to the animals, carrying Adam between his humps, while Gimel stayed with the alphabet, where he helped to make up words.

Of course Gimel and Gamal always remained good friends. But they stopped imitating each other and they did not go visiting quite so often.

Dalet
Helps Adam

For a long time the first man, Adam, and his wife, Eve, lived in the Garden of Eden. They were very happy in Eden. They had all the food they wanted. The climate was mild. They did not need a house to protect them. At night, they slept on beds of sweet pine needles under the trees.

At last Adam and Eve had to leave the Garden of Eden. It was not as comfortable anywhere as it had been in Eden. Sometimes it rained. Sometimes it snowed. When the winds blew from the north it was cold. When the winds blew from the south it was hot.

Adam and Eve found a cave to live in. The cave was more comfortable than it was out-of-doors, but it was not enough protection in bad weather. Eve was always catching cold. When it rained she sneezed and sniffled. When she wet her feet she caught the chills. She never felt just right.

One day Adam said, "I am going to build a house. You will be warm and comfortable if you have a house to live in."

Now Adam was the first man. So the house that Adam built was the first house in the world.

Adam went to the forest and cut down trees. Then he made four walls for his house. He put a roof on top of the walls and a floor underneath. When that was done, he put a chimney in the roof.

Adam stood back and admired his house. Eve admired it, too. It was a beautiful house.

Eve said, "Now I won't sneeze and sniffle

whenever it rains or snows. Our house will protect us in bad weather."

"Let's go inside and live in our house," said Adam.

They tried to go in, but the walls were in the way. They tried this way and that. They walked all around the house. They wracked their brains trying to think of some way to get in. But the walls were always in the way.

Adam and Eve were disappointed.

"What good is a house," they said, "if you can't get inside?"

Some animals who had been watching Adam build his house had suggestions.

"Perhaps you squeeze in through a crack," said the cat.

"Try boring a hole through the floor," said the mole.

"How about the chimney, Adam?" cried the monkey. "There's a hole in the chimney, so that must be the way you get in."

That was the best suggestion. They all decided that the hole in the chimney was for getting into the house. So Adam climbed onto the roof and lowered himself into his house through the chimney.

"How do you like it in your house?" the animals shouted down the chimney.

"It's very nice," said Adam. Then after a while he said, "But how do I get out?"

They had not thought of that.

"Can't you jump up?" asked the kangaroo.

"Try flying," said the owl.

"Crawl up the wall and onto the roof," said the fly.

"It's too high for jumping," said Adam. "And I can't fly and I can't crawl up the wall."

"Poor Adam," said Eve. "How will he ever get out?"

The animals thought and thought till they had a plan. The monkey climbed down the chimney. The bear sat on the roof and held onto the monkey's tail. And the elephant

stood on the ground and wrapped his trunk around the bear. Then the monkey pulled Adam up. The bear pulled the monkey out of the chimney and the elephant held onto the bear with all his might. That is how Adam got out of his house.

"I don't like it at all," said Adam when he was standing on the ground again. "It's too hard to get in and out of the house."

Now the letter Dalet, which looks like a door, heard about the trouble Adam was having with his new house. He decided to help him.

Away went Dalet to visit Adam and his new house. He found Adam and Eve and all the animals standing around the house wondering what to do next.

"Good day, Adam," said Dalet. "I hear you are having trouble with your new house."

"Yes," said Adam. "Eve and I can get into our house through the chimney. But it's very hard to get out."

"You're not supposed to go in and out

of your house through the chimney," said Dalet. "You should build a door."

"What's a door?" asked Adam.

"Something you walk in and out of."

"What does it look like?"

"It looks like me," said Dalet.

And he stood against one of the walls of the house.

"Make a door just like me," Dalet went on. "First cut a big hole in one of the walls. Put a piece of wood on hinges to swing back and forth. Then you have a door to use whenever you want to go in or out of your house."

Adam followed all of Dalet's directions. He cut a big hole in one of the walls. Then he put a piece of wood on hinges to swing back and forth. And he had a door that looked just like Dalet. When he wanted to go in and out of his house, he did not have to use the chimney. He went through the door, which was much easier. And Eve had a beautiful, snug house to keep her warm and comfortable whenever it rained or snowed.

Hey Wants Improvements

THE letter Dalet was telling the other letters of the Hebrew alphabet about Adam's new house.

"It has four walls," he said, "a roof, a floor, a chimney, and a door that looks like me."

"What about a window?" asked the letter Hey, who looked like a window. "Doesn't Adam's house have a window, too?"

"No," said Dalet, "it hasn't."

"But it should have," said Hey. "Adam

should have a window for fresh air and sun-shine."

And Hey went off to tell Adam.

Adam and Eve were in their new house when Hey knocked on the door that looked like Dalet.

"Who is it?" called Adam.

"It's the letter Hey."

Adam opened his new door.

"Good morning, Adam," said Hey. "I see you have a nice new house. But it has no window."

"What's a window?" asked Adam.

"A window is something that looks like me," Hey explained.

"Where do I put it?" asked Adam.

"You make a hole in the wall," Hey said, "and then —"

"No," Adam interrupted. "I am not going to put any more holes in my nice new walls. I made one hole for a door, and that is enough."

"But Adam," said Hey, "you need a window for fresh air and sunshine."

"When we want fresh air and sunshine," said Adam, "we go out-of-doors."

And no matter what Hey said, Adam refused to cut any more holes in his new walls.

Hey waited until Adam's children grew up and built houses of their own. They built walls and chimneys and doors and ceilings and floors. But no windows.

As soon as their houses were built Hey went to see them about windows.

"What's a window?" they asked.

"A hole in the wall for fresh air and sunshine," said Hey.

"Father Adam has no holes in his wall for air and sunshine," they said, "and we don't want any either."

Many, many years passed. Thousands of people were living on the earth and building houses. But none of them wanted windows. Their houses were all like the house that Adam had built.

Hey was becoming discouraged. He was just about to give up when he heard of a new

house that someone was building. It was a
boathouse, an ark. The man who was building
it was called Noah. Noah and his family
and many animals were going to live in it

for a long time, because there was going to be a flood.

Hey went to see Noah.

31

Father Noah and his wife, Mother Noah, were standing in front of their ark. It had three floors and a door, but no windows. In front of the ark, the animals were lined up — Mr. and Mrs. Lion, Mr. and Mrs. Bear, Mr. and Mrs. Kangaroo and many, many others. There were two of every kind of animal, all waiting to get into the ark. Father Noah checked their names off his long list. His three sons, Shem, Ham and Japheth, kept the animals from pushing each other out of line.

When Hey saw Noah he went running down the long row of animals to get to him quickly.

"Get in line," Shem called to Hey. "You must wait for your turn."

"But I want to see Father Noah," said Hey.

"Everyone wants to see Father Noah," said Ham. "Get in line."

Hey got in line. He was the very last, right behind the zebras. They turned around and looked at him.

"Where's your wife?" asked Mr. Zebra. "You can't get into the ark without your wife."

"I haven't got a wife," said Hey, "and I'm not going into the ark."

The line of animals moved forward very slowly. Noah checked them off his list and they entered the ark. At last it was Hey's turn.

"Your name?" said Noah.

Don't you recognize me, Father Noah?" asked Hey.

Noah put on his spectacles.

"Upon my word," he said, "you are the letter Hey. What are you doing here? Don't you know there's going to be a flood?"

"Father Noah," said Hey, "I think you ought to put a window in your ark."

"A window?" said Father Noah. "What for?"

"It's going to rain and rain," said Hey, "and you won't be able to go out-of-doors for air. How are you and all the animals going to stay healthy? And how are you going to see what is happening outside? And how will you know when it stops raining?"

Noah said he didn't know.

"And besides," Hey went on, "all the houses on earth are going to be drowned. Yours will be the only one left. If your ark has windows, people will all put windows in their houses when they build new ones after the flood."

Father Noah scratched his head and thought the matter over. Then he said, "All right, I shall put windows in my ark."

And he called his three sons and told them to make copies of the letter Hey in the walls of the ark, one on each floor.

Hey was very happy. At last there was a house with windows.

All the other houses were drowned. Only the ark was left. After the flood people built their houses with improvements. They all put windows in their walls to let in the fresh air and sunshine.

How Vav's Cousin
Saved the Jews

ONE DAY the letters of the Hebrew alphabet sat talking about themselves.

"My name means hook," said the letter Vav proudly, "and I look like a hook. A hook is a very useful thing."

The letters agreed that a hook could be very useful. It was something people hung their hats and coats on. But Vav said that hooks could be more important than that.

"My Cousin the Hook," Vav told them, "once saved the Jews."

The letters stared at Vav.

"When?" asked Aleph. "When did your Cousin the Hook save the Jews?"

"When they were slaves in Egypt," said Vav.

"I always thought that Moses saved the Jews," said Bet.

"My cousin helped Moses," said Vav quietly.

And Vav told the story of how his Cousin the Hook helped Moses save the Jews.

"The Jews were slaves in Egypt for many years. They made bricks in the hot sun and built palaces and monuments. The harder they worked, the crueler did Pharaoh of Egypt become.

"At last Moses came to free his people. He brought swarms of grasshoppers upon Egypt to punish Pharaoh and his task-masters. He brought frogs and toads. They were a nuisance. He brought pitch blackness, so that the Egyptians could not see where they were going, even in the daytime. They stumbled all over each other.

"Pharaoh could not stand it any longer. He told Moses to take the Jews out of Egypt.

"The Jews had not been out of Egypt very long when Pharaoh changed his mind. He decided to bring them back to build more palaces and monuments.

"Pharaoh climbed into his chariot and blew his trumpet. His soldiers came running from their barracks. They mounted their swift horses. Then away they went to bring back the Jews, with Pharaoh leading the way.

"Pharaoh rode in his fine chariot in front of the army. All his officers rode behind him — the generals, colonels, majors, captains, and the first and second lieutenants. They rode in chariots, like Pharaoh. The rest of the army rode on horses.

"The Jews had no chariots or horses. They were traveling on foot. Pharaoh's army traveled much faster. Soon Pharaoh saw them from afar.

" 'Faster!' he shouted to his generals.

" 'Faster!' the generals shouted to the officers.

" 'Faster!' the officers shouted to the rest of the army.

"They went faster.

"Pharaoh whipped his horses. They sped forward. Behind him came his great army, their javelins and shields glittering in the sun. The wheels of the chariots turned. The horses' hooves beat like thunder on the ground. Faster and faster they went. Nearer and nearer they came to the long procession of Jews marching toward the Red Sea.

"Pharaoh lashed his horses till they shot forward like streaks of lightning. They came to a hill. Up the hill Pharaoh's horses galloped, with the Egyptian army close behind. Up, up, up they went. And when they got to the top of the hill —"

The letter Vav leaned back. All the other letters leaned forward.

"What happened?" they asked.

38

"On top of the hill," said Vav, "there was a big rock. Pharaoh's chariot bumped over the rock. Then, out fell my Cousin the Hook."

"Fell out of what?" asked Gimel.

"He fell out of the axle that held the wheels of Pharaoh's chariot. Out came my cousin. Out came the wheels. Down went the axle. Over went the chariot. And out tumbled Pharaoh of Egypt.

"He rolled down the hill to the very bottom. And there he lay. The generals and colonels and majors and captains and lieutenants jumped out of their chariots. They ran down the hill to pick him up. Pharaoh was lying 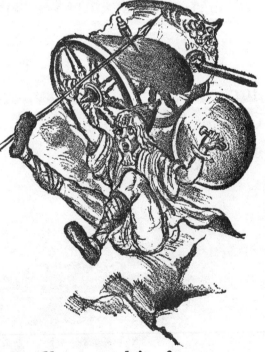 in a ditch, with dirt all over his face.

"They picked him up carefully and carried him to the top of the hill. Then they set him down on the ground. They fussed over him for a long time. The army doctor examined him for injuries. Pharaoh was covered with bruises and bumps. He had a terrible headache. The doctor advised him to rest.

"In the meantime, the Jews got to the Red Sea. By the time Pharaoh caught up with them, they were safe.

"And all because of my Cousin the Hook."

When Vav finished his story the letters agreed that if it had not been for Vav's Cousin the Hook, the Jews might still be slaves in Egypt.

Zayín
is
Helpful

IT WAS a bright, sunny morning. A hawk was flying through the mountains in search of food. On top of one mountain the hawk saw a bird's egg. The egg was speckled red and green and yellow, and it was so big that it reached the clouds.

The hawk had never seen such a giant egg before. Away he flew to tell the other birds about it. In a little while all the birds were on their way to see the great, speckled egg that lay on top of the mountain.

The eagle came, and the raven, the parrot,

the linnet, the canary, the hummingbird, the wren, the robin, the starling, the lark, the oriole, the nightingale, the swallow, the dove. All the birds in the bird kingdom came flying to see the biggest egg in the world.

When they reached the mountain top they formed a great circle around the egg and waited for it to hatch. They waited all day and all night. Early the next morning, as the sun rose in the sky, the egg began to rock slowly from side to side. Then the speckled shell cracked open. Out stepped a bird. It had a bright yellow body, red wings, and a green and purple crest on its head. The bird was so big its head reached the sky. All the other birds, even the eagle, looked like flies as they stood around it.

"Good morning," the birds said.

"Good morning," answered the newly-hatched giant.

"Where is your mother?" asked the hawk.

"I have no mother," said the giant bird. "I am the first bird of my kind."

"Are you hungry?" asked the dove.

"Yes," said the newcomer, ruffling his feathers. "I would like to eat."

With a flutter of many wings the birds flew off to bring him food. They came back with thousands of worms. But all the worms

were just enough for a nibble for the giant bird. The birds flew off for more worms. It took a long time to feed the giant, but at last he was satisfied. He said he couldn't eat another thing.

"You are the biggest bird there ever was," said the wren. "And you can eat more than any of us. You should be our king."

All the birds agreed. They cried, "Hurrah! Long live King—"

But that was as far as they got.

"What's your name?" asked the eagle.

"I don't have a name," said the new bird. "I was just hatched."

"We can't have a king without a name," said the raven. "Would you like to use mine?"

"Or mine?" asked the swallow.

A quarrel broke out among the birds. Each wanted the king-bird to take his name, so that he would be his relative and get special favors. But the giant bird refused to take any of their names.

"I want my own," he said. "How do you get a name?"

"Go to the alphabet," said the robin. "The letters will help you."

The giant bird flew off to the Hebrew alphabet to get a name.

When the letters of the alphabet saw him flying toward them they were very frightened. His outspread wings covered the sky, and the land below lay in deep shadow. Never had the letters seen such a big bird before. They stood close together, trembling. That is, all but one of them.

That one was not Aleph. Aleph was frightened when the giant bird spoke to him.

"Will you help me find a name?" the bird asked him.

"If you don't mind," said Aleph timidly, "I have an appointment to finish a word I began yesterday. And I don't like to keep words waiting. Some other time."

And off he went to keep his appointment.

The bird turned to Bet.

"Will you please help me find a name?" he asked.

"I . . ." said Bet, "well . . . we . . . you see . . . ."

And Bet just lost his tongue and could not say another word.

"What's the matter with them?" thought the bird. "They act so strangely, they frighten me. But I must have a name."

And he turned to Gimel.

"Who, me?" said Gimel. "Sorry, old bird, but I already have an animal relative, Gamal the Camel, out in the Great Desert."

The bird turned to Dalet. But Dalet suddenly remembered something he had to do.

"It's very important," he said as he ran off. "In the meantime, ask Hey. He knows all about names and things."

"I don't know about names and things," Hey told the bird. "And I really don't see how I can be of any use. I'm already in so many words, I just won't be able to manage . . . ."

It was Vav's turn.

"A fine name *I* would make," Vav scoffed at himself. "Just look at me, not much to look at. Why not try the letter Zayin?"

Now Zayin, whose name means weapon, was a bold, fearless letter. He was not afraid of anything. Zayin was keen as a sword, and whenever a letter got into trouble, he came to Zayin to help him out.

Zayin looked the great bird straight in the eye and asked, "What can I do to help you?"

"I need a name," said the bird, "and I wish you would help me find one. Everyone has a name, except me, because I was just hatched."

"Would you like me to be in your name?" asked Zayin.

"If you please," said the bird. "I'd be very grateful."

47

"All right," said Zayin, "you can have me in your name. In fact...." Zayin had an idea. "In fact," he said, "you can have me in your name twice, at the beginning and at the end!"

The giant bird was grateful.

"Thank you very much," he said.

"Your name shall be Ziz, King of the Birds!" said Zayin.

And all the letters of the alphabet, happy that Ziz had found his name, cried, "Long live Ziz, King of the Birds!"

And that is how the biggest bird that ever lived got his name.

Het

Goes Fishing

THE letter Het, who looks like a fishnet, once decided to go fishing. Away he went, thinking of all the fish he would catch for the alphabet's dinner. As he went along he sang a little song to himself:

Some trout for Aleph, Bet and Gimel,
Dalet would like some flounder,
A bit of perch for Zayin, Hey,
And cod to make Vav rounder.

When Het got to the sea he looked about him. Fishermen sat in boats and threw nets into the water. When the nets were full of fish the fishermen pulled them up and emptied the fish into their boats. Then they threw the nets back into the sea again.

"It's very easy," thought Het. "I just get into the water, like a fishnet, and catch some fish. I think I'll catch twenty-two, one for each letter of the alphabet."

Het put one foot into the water. It was very cold. He took out the first foot and put in the other. The water was just as cold. Het decided to jump in, the way the fishnets did.

Het went back a few steps, then he ran forward and dived headlong into the sea. The water splashed over him and he got wet from top to bottom. Het moved his legs about as hard as he could, trying to keep on top of the waves.

"If I could only swim," thought Het. "How am I ever going to catch fish if I can't swim?"

A big flounder swam by. His fins moved

gracefully back and forth in the water. The flounder looked at Het with his glassy eyes. Het was frightened. He tried to get out of the way. The flounder came closer and opened his mouth. Just then, down came a fishnet and scooped the flounder up out of the water.

"If I don't look out," said Het to himself, "I'll be caught in a fishnet, too."

Het moved his feet and tried to tread water, like a duck. He even pretended he had fins, like a real fish. No matter what he did, he could not swim.

A fat perch came along. The perch's mouth was open.

"Don't swallow me!" cried Het.

The perch, who had not even noticed Het, closed his mouth around a big fly that was sitting on top of the water, and swam away.

Just then a huge wave lifted Het on its crest and carried him far out to sea.

"How will I ever get back?" thought Het. "Oh ... what's this coming now?"

It was a whale. The whale swam straight toward Het. It moved like a black mountain through the water, nearer and nearer, darker and darker.

Het tried with all his might to get out of the way. He splashed and he kicked. He jumped up and down, and he twisted and turned. But instead of moving, Het seemed to be staying in one spot.

The whale opened his mouth. It was like a great dark cave.

"Help!" cried Het. "Help!" Then Het was silent. The next thing he said was, "Where am I?"

He was inside the whale. It was very dark. No windows, no doors. Just whale, wherever Het looked.

Het was sorry he had ever gone fishing.

"Let me out!" he cried. "Let me out!"

And Het ran up and down the inside of the whale, trying to find a crack somewhere to get out.

Now, the whale was ticklish. He had never had anyone run up and down his inside before. He plunged deep into the water, hoping to get rid of the tickling that way. Down fell Het, rolling and bumping from side to side. The whale dove deeper into the sea. Het pitched and tumbled up and down, back and forth, like a rubber ball. Up came the whale to the surface of the sea. Up and down and round went Het.

At last the whale could not stand the tickling any longer. He filled his mouth with water and blew with all his might. Out came Het on a great geyser of water, out of the inside of the whale.

Het went flying into the air. He flew so high that when he looked down the sea seemed like a saucer of water below him. Just as he was about to go tumbling down again an eagle flew by and caught him in his strong beak.

The eagle looked at Het with his beady eyes.

"Hmm," he said, "you don't look like
a worm. What are you?"

"I'm a letter of the Hebrew alphabet," said Het.

"Letters don't fly in the air," said the eagle. "We'll soon find out what you are."

And the eagle flew off with Het in his beak.

They flew over the sea, over the land, till they came to a mountain. On top of the mountain was the home of Ziz, King of the Birds. Ziz was perched on a crag, his head reaching the sky. About him stood the birds of the bird kingdom.

The eagle settled at the feet of King Ziz.

"O great King," said the eagle, "see what I have found. Perhaps it is a new kind of flying worm."

And he held Het up for Ziz to see.

Ziz bent down and looked at Het curiously.

"You look like a fishnet," said Ziz. "But you're too small for that. What are you?"

"I'm a Hebrew letter," said Het. "Please let me go back to the alphabet."

"You're not Aleph," said Ziz, "and you're not Bet, and you're not — you must be a fishnet."

"I'm Het," said Het. Then he added eagerly, "I'm Zayin's next door neighbor. You can ask Zayin who I am."

Ziz thought for a while, then he turned to the swallow.

"Go and bring Zayin," he said.

The swallow flew off and soon returned, carrying sharp little Zayin in his beak.

"Friend Zayin," said Ziz, "do you know this fishnet?"

Zayin looked at Het, then he said, "He's not a fishnet. He only looks like one. That's Het, my neighbor."

Ziz turned and spoke to Het.

"Go back to the alphabet," he told him. "And see that you don't go gallivanting around any more."

Ziz appointed two doves to bring Zayin and Het back to the alphabet. On the way home Het told Zayin about his great adventure at sea.

And that was the end of Het's fishing. He never went down to the sea to fish again because, he told the letters of the alphabet, they probably would not like fish for dinner anyway.

Only Zayin knew the real reason. But Zayin had promised his friend Het never to tell anyone. And he never did.

Tet Goes
on a Journey

THE letters of the Hebrew alphabet were watching the Jews march through the Great Desert, away from the land of Egypt. There were so many of them they reached for miles and miles over the desert sand. Some rode on donkeys. Some rode on camels. Most of them walked. At the head of the long procession went Moses, leading his people toward the land of Canaan.

"Look at my friend Gamal the Camel," said the letter Gimel. "He's carrying an old man between his humps."

"And look at those fine swords the guards have in their belts," said Zayin. "They look like me."

The letter Tet, who looks like a basket, was interested in baskets.

"There's a fine one made of straw." He pointed to a basket a woman was carrying on her head. "It's just right for going to the market. And there's a basket made of bulrushes," Tet went on. "It's for a baby to sleep in."

Tet was silent for a moment, then he said anxiously, "Didn't Moses tell the Jews to take all their possessions with them?"

"Yes," said the letters, "he did."

"Then where's the basket the Baby Moses slept in when he floated on the Nile River?" asked Tet.

None of the letters knew.

"They should have taken the basket with them," said Tet. "They should not have left it for the Egyptians."

The letters looked carefully at the things

the Jews were carrying with them from Egypt. They saw tents and blankets and jars of food and jugs of oil. They saw toys and fine clothes and leather sandals. They saw red baskets and green baskets and yellow baskets. But there was no sign anywhere of the basket of the Baby Moses. The Jews were not taking it out of Egypt.

Tet did not like that at all.

"I'm going to Egypt," he said. "I'm going to find out what happened to that basket."

And Tet rushed off to Egypt to find the basket of the Baby Moses.

First he went to the Sphinx that sat like a giant of stone in the Great Desert.

"O Sphinx," said the letter Tet, "they say you know many secrets, though you are

always silent. Can you tell me where to look for the basket of the Baby Moses?"

The eyes of the Sphinx stared straight ahead. The lips of stone remained closed. But from the depths of the Sphinx came a voice like the rumbling of a deep volcano.

"I know many secrets," said the voice of the Sphinx, "but I do not know the secret of the basket of the Baby Moses. Go to the pyramids. On the walls of the pyramids are the stories of the Pharaohs who have died. The stories are written in the letters of the Egyptian alphabet. Ask the letters of the Egyptian alphabet. Perhaps they can

tell you the story of the basket of the Baby Moses."

The voice of the Sphinx was silent. The giant statue stared out over the hot sands of the desert. And Tet walked on to the mighty pyramids.

There he found the cold gray tombs of the Pharaohs of Egypt. On the walls of the tombs, engraved in the letters of the Egyptian alphabet, were the stories of the Pharaohs who had died.

"Tell me, O Egyptian Alphabet," said Tet, "where can I find the basket of the Baby Moses?"

The letters of the Egyptian alphabet looked down at Tet from the stone walls.

"We do not know," they said. "On the walls of these tombs are only the stories of the Pharaohs of Egypt. Go to the palace of Pharaoh. There you will find the library of papyrus scrolls. On these scrolls are written all the stories of Egypt. Ask the scrolls for the story of the basket of the Baby Moses."

Tet went on to the palace of Pharaoh. There he found a great chamber filled with papyrus scrolls. There were large scrolls and small scrolls. Each scroll had a story written upon it. One had the story of Joseph, who had saved Egypt from famine. One had the story of the Nile River and how it overflowed its banks and made the land fertile. Another had the story of the pyramids and of the silent Sphinx. And another had the story of the beautiful Princess Thermutis who had taken the Baby Moses from the Nile River.

"Tell me, O Papyrus Scrolls," said Tet, "do you know the story of the basket of the Baby Moses?"

The scrolls rustled on the shelves of the great chamber. Then they spoke in voices that crackled like dry leaves.

"No one has ever written the story of the basket of the Baby Moses," they said. And they were silent.

But one of the smaller scrolls said to the letter Tet, "I am made of papyrus reeds that grow along the edge of the Nile River. When I was still a clump of reeds growing beside the river, I saw Miriam put the basket that held her brother Moses into a bed of bulrushes. Follow the road from the palace till you come to the Nile River. There you will find the bed of bulrushes. Perhaps they can tell you what has become of the basket of the Baby Moses."

Tet left the library of papyrus scrolls and followed the road from the palace till he came

to the Nile River. There he found the bed of bulrushes.

"O Bulrushes," said Tet, "can you tell me where to find the basket of the Baby Moses?"

The bulrushes swayed gently back and forth in the breeze that blew over the Nile. Then they spoke in their soft, murmuring voices.

"The basket of the Baby Moses was made of bulrushes like us," they said. "But we do not know what happened to it. When Princess Thermutis took Moses from the basket, the river current snatched it up and carried it away. Ask the river current where the basket is."

Tet turned to the river current that swept along between the fertile banks.

"O River Current," said Tet, "can you tell me what happened to the basket of the Baby Moses?"

The current flowed past the river-bank as it spoke in its deep, watery voice.

"Come," said the current, "I will take you to the basket."

Tet mounted the current. He rode swiftly on the surface of the water, past lotus plants and papyrus reeds. He was carried around little islands fringed with lilies and rushes. Between rows of stately palm trees, Tet sailed down the Nile River.

The rays of the sun glittered on the face of the water. Fish swam by, and birds and insects circled overhead. Tet looked everywhere for the basket of the Baby Moses, deep within the water and along the riverbanks. But there was no sign of it anywhere.

At last the river turned, then opened with a wide sweep. A golden stretch of water lay between low, peaceful banks. Bright-winged birds dipped and circled over the shining river. On the grassy banks grew every tree of the land of Egypt, the date tree and the olive tree, the apricot tree and the walnut tree and the lemon tree. The shadows of the trees reached into the water like the columns of cool palaces.

Against one bank of the river grew a bed of bulrushes. The bulrushes were tall and green, and they swayed gently back and forth in the breeze. And as they stirred, their rustling voice sang a soft lullaby.

Tet listened to the song of the bulrushes. It was the lullaby of Yochebed, the mother of Moses. Long, long ago, she had sung it to the Baby Moses when she had placed him in the basket of bulrushes.

At last Tet knew the secret of the basket of the Baby Moses. The river current had carried it to the most beautiful spot on the Nile River. There the bulrushes of the basket had unwound, one by one, and had sunk back into the bed of the river. And there they remained, singing to the peaceful waters and to the birds and to the trees the lullaby that Moses had heard when he was a baby.

Tet was happy. He returned to the alphabet and told the letters the secret of the basket of the Baby Moses.

Yod Becomes Important

THE letter Yod was the Tom Thumb of the Hebrew alphabet. But he did not like being Tom Thumb. He wanted to be big and important, like the other letters.

"I'm no bigger than a dot with a tail stuck on," he complained. "Just look at me."

The letters looked at Yod. They did not see anything wrong with his looks. They thought he was a bit delicate, perhaps — but there was nothing wrong with that.

The letters all tried to comfort Yod.

"Yod is important for all kinds of words," said Aleph.

"Besides," said Bet, "how about numbers? I stand for the number two because I am only the second letter in the alphabet."

"And look at me," said Gimel. "I only stand for three because I am the third letter."

"While you're the tenth letter, so you stand for the number ten, even though you are small," added Dalet.

But Yod was not interested in arithmetic. All he cared about was size and importance.

Yod decided to run away.

"I won't stay here and be the smallest letter in the alphabet," thought Yod. "If I run away, perhaps I shall meet a big adventure that will make me important."

One day, while the other letters were busy making up words, little Yod slipped out of the alphabet and ran away into the big world.

He walked down a long, winding road, looking for adventure. At first he was happy, for the sun was bright and the birds were singing. But soon a great creature came along that Yod had never seen before.

The creature was an ant. He almost frightened Yod out of his wits. This ant happened to be very rude.

"Get out of my way, Tom Thumb," he snapped. "I'm in a hurry."

Instead of telling the ant to get out of the way himself, Yod scampered off to the side of the road, where he waited till the ant had passed.

Yod was about to walk on when a purple butterfly rose from a goldenrod. The butterfly circled about the goldenrod, then flew over Yod's head and brushed him with her soft wings, almost throwing him to the ground. Yod dashed behind a pebble for safety, and the butterfly fluttered on to a field of daisies.

"The world is a dangerous place," thought Yod.

When the butterfly was out of sight, Yod came out from behind the pebble. He looked

to the right and he looked to the left. Then he marched bravely down the winding road.

Suddenly a huge monster came hopping across the road. He had long legs, bulging eyes, and two long swords sticking out of the sides of his head. When the monster saw Yod he stopped and looked him over carefully.

"Who — are — you?" quaked poor Yod.

"I'm a grasshopper," said the monster, "and I think I'll eat you for dinner."

"You can't eat me," said Yod. "I'm a letter of the alphabet."

"What's the alphabet?" asked the grass-hopper.

"Twenty-two letters," said Yod. "And we're very important. We make words."

"Then why aren't you in the alphabet instead of here?" asked the grasshopper.

"I'm looking for adventure," Yod explained.

"Hmm," said the grasshopper grumpily. "All right, then. I'll have to find something else for dinner."

The grasshopper hopped away and Yod turned into a field to look for adventure.

He picked his way through the towering blades of grass. He climbed over thistles and clover. He pushed on through forests of daisies and buttercups.

Suddenly the skies grew dark. Great black clouds moved over the trees. The crickets and locusts began to chirp in their shrill voices. Yod had never heard such a din before. He decided to get out of the field

as quickly as he could and onto the open road, where it was quiet.

Yod had only taken a few steps when — splash! A big raindrop fell from the dark sky. The raindrop fell on Yod and covered him from head to toe.

"Help!" cried Yod. "I'm drowning!"

He spluttered and splashed his way out of the raindrop. Then he dashed under a blade of grass, where he could be safe and dry. Here Yod lay, while the rain spattered on flowers and grass and made rivers all around him.

But at last the rain stopped. The sky grew bright and clear again and a rainbow of many colors appeared. The rainbow curved in a beautiful arch from one horizon to the other.

Yod crawled out from under the blade of grass.

"Maybe I'd better go back home," he thought. "The letters must be lonesome without me."

There was a sudden whirring over Yod's head. Then a strong wind swept him up from the ground and carried him high into the air. Twisting and turning dizzily, Yod flew through the air like a whirling leaf.

"Why did I ever leave home?" moaned Yod.

Up went the wind, carrying Yod toward the blue sky. At last the wind dropped him on top of the rainbow.

"Well," thought Yod, "that wasn't so bad. I hope I'm safe up here."

Yod stood on his high perch and looked about. Far below him he saw houses and trees and barns. They looked like little black dots from the crest of the rainbow. And the great seas and oceans seemed like tiny blue lakes.

"Things don't look so big from up here," cried Yod in delight. "I think I'll live in the sky forever."

Poor Yod. At that moment he slipped. Plunging and spinning, he slid down the curve of the rainbow. He went bouncing from color to color. From Red to Orange to Yellow to Green to Blue to Violet. Down he went. By the time he reached Violet he was at the end of the rainbow. With a great bump, he landed on the earth.

Yod got up and looked around. He was standing in the Great Desert near a mountain. Many people were gathered at the foot of the mountain.

On the mountain side stood a man.

"Why, that's Moses," said Yod.

Moses was holding tablets of stone in his hands. Yod came closer to the mountain. He wanted to hear what Moses was saying.

"You were slaves in the land of Egypt," said Moses. "But now you are free men. You are going to live in a beautiful land called Canaan. There you will be happy, if you are kind and just to each other."

Moses held up the tablets of stone so that all the people could see them.

"On these tablets," he said, "are ten laws

which will teach you to be just and kind. These laws are called the Ten Commandments."

Yod could hardly believe his ears.

"Ten Commandments," he thought happily. "And I stand for the number ten. Then I am important after all."

"In years to come," Moses was talking to the people again, "you will give these Ten Commandments to all the world, and all nations shall learn to love truth and justice."

Moses came down from the mountain side. The people moved on behind their leader toward the rich land of Canaan. And a very excited, important Yod returned to his place in the alphabet.

How Kaf Found
Jewels for
Solomon's Crown

SOLOMON, King of the Jews, was the wisest man who ever lived. He knew the languages of all living things. But Solomon was not only wise. He had great power. Because of his power he was master of the birds, the beasts, the fish, the spirits and the demons.

When Solomon first came to his throne in the city of Jerusalem, he looked in his treasure house for jewels to set in his crown. There were golden caskets filled with gems and precious stones of every kind. But none of these was beautiful enough for the crown of Solomon, wisest of kings.

A wide search began for jewels for Solomon's crown. Throughout the kingdom, men dug the earth and the hills for precious stones. Solomon sent messengers to foreign lands, offering great rewards for rare jewels. Monarchs and princes sent their most valued gems to Jerusalem. But Solomon was not satisfied.

"The jewels of my crown," he said, "must be the most beautiful that man has ever seen."

Now the letters of the Hebrew alphabet were very much interested in whatever happened in the kingdom of the Jews. King Solomon was a just and kind ruler, and the letters wanted him to have a beautiful crown.

One day the letter Kaf said, "I am the first letter of the word Keter, which means crown. I shall find the jewels for Solomon's crown."

And Kaf went to Ziz, King of the Birds.

"O King Ziz," said Kaf, "I am looking for jewels for the crown of King Solomon. Will you help me find them?"

"I will help you," said Ziz.

And Ziz called all the birds of his kingdom.

From every mountain and from every forest tree they came. They came over land and sea. They came in great flocks, so that the sky was dark with their wings.

When all the birds stood before him, Ziz spoke to them.

"I have called you," he said, "to help the letter Kaf find jewels for Solomon's crown. Search every mountain. Scour the peaks and

the precipices and the canyons below. And when you have found the treasures that the mountains hold, bring them to me."

The birds flew off. They searched the mountains of the earth. They scoured the peaks and the precipices. They flew through the deep canyons and over the green pastures. At last they returned with the gems they had found and placed them at the feet of Ziz.

"Here are the jewels of the Kingdom of the Birds," said Ziz to the letter Kaf. "Choose

any among them for the crown of King Solomon."

Kaf gazed at the heap of gleaming jewels. There were precious stones of every color of the rainbow. There were stones that glowed gently like the early dawn, and there were stones that were radiant as the sun. But the most beautiful gem of all was a sapphire. It was as blue and clear as a cloudless sky on a summer day.

"Of all the gems in the Kingdom of the Birds," said Kaf, "this sapphire is the most beautiful."

Ziz called the eagle.

"Take this sapphire to the tree on the hillside where the shepherd plays his flute. In the morning the shepherd will find the jewel and he will take it to King Solomon."

The eagle bore the sapphire to the hillside where the shepherd played his flute. He laid it under the tree, as Ziz had commanded.

And Kaf went to Leviathan, King of the Fish.

Leviathan lived in the deep, cool chambers of the sea. He was three hundred miles long from end to end. His eyes and fins were so bright that they made the bottom of the sea as light as day. When Leviathan was angry his breath grew hot and the water bubbled and boiled for miles around.

Kaf entered the palace of the King of the Sea. In a vast, green chamber, upon a coral throne, sat Leviathan.

"O King Leviathan," said Kaf, "I am looking for jewels for Solomon's crown. Will you help me find them?"

"I will help you," said Leviathan.

And Leviathan summoned all the fish of his kingdom.

From the seven seas and from the gulfs and from the rivers of the earth the fish came swimming to Leviathan's throne. The whale came, and the swordfish, the salmon, the trout, the bass, the perch, the flounder, the mackerel, the cod. The shellfish came too — the lobster, the clam, the oyster. And the sea lions came, and the dolphins, who were half man and half fish, and the sea-goats, with horns on their heads.

When all the subjects of his kingdom were before him, Leviathan spoke.

"Go forth," he said, "to every corner of the Kingdom of the Sea, and look for jewels for King Solomon's crown. When you have found the gems that the waters hold, bring them to me."

The fish swam off and searched the waters for jewels. They looked in the deep sea caverns. They searched the gulfs and the inlets and the winding waterways. They followed the currents along the shores of the continents. They swam the icy seas of the North and the warm waters of the Equator. And they searched the ocean floor.

Then they brought all the jewels they had found to Leviathan.

"These are the gems of the Kingdom of the Sea," Leviathan said to Kaf. "Choose any among them for the crown of King Solomon."

Kaf looked at the rich gems of the Kingdom of the Sea. He saw jewels whose color was clear as water on a sunny day. He saw jewels that were purple, like waves in an angry storm. There were gems that glittered coldly, like crystals of ice, and green gems, whose color was like soft moss. But the loveliest jewel of all was a pearl. It was as white and pure as the driven snow, yet in it were the reflections of all the colors of the Kingdom of the Sea.

"This pearl," said Kaf, "is the most beautiful of all the gems of the Kingdom of the Sea."

Leviathan called the swordfish.

"Cast this pearl up on the shore of the sea," he said. "In the morning, when the fisherman comes to fish, he will find it and take it to King Solomon."

The swordfish took the pearl and cast it up on the shore of the sea.

And Kaf went to Ashmodai, King of the Demons.

Ashmodai lived in a huge cavern deep in the Dark Mountains. His body was like a man's, but his feet were those of a bird. Ashmodai's eyes shone like lightning, and from his nostrils a red flame came forth.

Kaf entered the cavern of Ashmodai. Wrapped in darkness, on a black throne of ebony, sat the King of Demons.

"O King Ashmodai," said Kaf, "I am looking for jewels for Solomon's crown. Will you help me find them?"

"I will help you," said Ashmodai.

And he called the demons of his kingdom.

All the demons came hurrying to the cavern of Ashmodai in the Dark Mountains. They came from the gloomy forests and from secret hollows never seen by man. From the four corners of the earth, they sped to the throne of their master.

When all the demons stood before him in his vast cavern, Ashmodai spoke.

"Go forth," he said, "and look for jewels for King Solomon's crown. Search the deep forests and the secret places of the earth. When you have found the rarest treasures that the earth holds, bring them to me."

The demons went off to search for jewels. They searched the gloomy forests. They sought out the bottomless chasms and the hidden places of the earth. At last they returned, bearing the gems they had found.

"These are the rarest treasures the earth holds," said Ashmodai to the letter Kaf. "Choose any among them for the crown of Solomon."

Kaf looked at the gems that lay in a mound before the throne of Ashmodai. They glowed like a heap of burning embers — crimson, and deep violet, sparkling green and soft blue, and the white glitter of diamond. Their radiance pierced the darkness of the vast cavern like the rays of a thousand suns.

The most beautiful jewel of all was a ruby. It was a rich, glowing red, yet its heart was deep as the forest, and cool as the mountain spring.

"This ruby," said Kaf, "is the most beautiful of all the gems of the earth."

Ashmodai turned to one of his demons.

"Take this ruby to the forest," he said,

"and lay it under the oak tree near the woodcutter's house. When the woodcutter awakes in the morning he will find it and bring it to King Solomon."

The demon took the ruby and laid it under the oak tree near the woodcutter's house.

And Kaf returned to the alphabet.

The next morning the shepherd who played his flute on the hillside found the sapphire. The fisherman who went down to

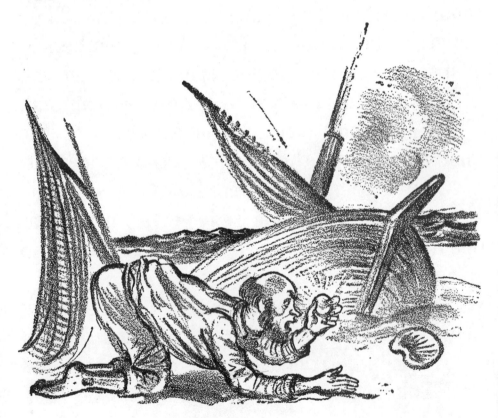

the sea found the pearl. The woodcutter who
lived near the oak tree found the ruby.

They brought the jewels to King Solomon
in Jerusalem. Solomon gazed upon them and
he was pleased.

"These shall be the jewels of my crown,"
he said, "for they are the most beautiful
that man has ever seen."

Lamed
Visits Leviathan

THE letter Lamed was the tallest letter of
the Hebrew alphabet. The other letters
looked up to Lamed because he could see
over their heads. When he stood among them
and looked to the right and to the left, he
was tall and handsome, like a big chief. The
letters called him their Letter-in-Chief.

Leviathan, King of the Fish, was jealous
of Lamed.

"Lamed is more important than I am,"
he would grumble.

"But Lamed is only ruler of twenty-one letters," his counselors would say, "while you, O Leviathan, are king of millions and millions of fish."

"Yet I'm not half as important as Lamed," said Leviathan. "For letters make words and words make books and everybody reads books. So Lamed is really King of Everybody. And I am only King of the Fish."

The more Leviathan thought about Lamed, the angrier he became. And when Leviathan was angry his breath grew hot and the water about him bubbled and boiled. All the little fish swam out of danger to the surface of the sea.

Leviathan sat on his throne and sulked. When he got tired of sulking, he decided to do something about it. He thought and thought. He plotted and planned. At last his plot was ready.

Leviathan called for a flying fish.

"Go to the Hebrew alphabet," said Leviathan, "and tell Lamed, Letter-in-Chief, that I, Leviathan, King of the Fish, invite him to visit me as my royal guest."

The flying fish departed at once for the Hebrew alphabet. He found the Letter-in-Chief standing in front of the alphabet, calling the roll.

"Aleph."

"Here."

"Bet."

"Here."

"Gimel, Dalet."

"Here, here."

The flying fish interrupted the roll call.

"O Letter-in-Chief Lamed," he said, "King Leviathan invites you to visit him as his royal guest in the Kingdom of the Sea."

Now Lamed loved visiting, especially kings. He was always looking for hints on how to rule and he thought he could learn a few things from Leviathan. So he said good-by to his friends in the alphabet and hurried off to King Leviathan.

Leviathan could not keep Lamed in his

kingdom by force. He could not put him in chains because he did not have any. And he could not lock him up because there were no doors. So he pretended he loved Lamed and he made his visit very pleasant. He hoped that Lamed would never want to return to his alphabet.

Leviathan gave Lamed many gifts — tinted shells, coral, and strange plants that grew at the bottom of the sea. The sea-goats danced for him and the dolphins sang him water music. Lamed was so delighted with the Kingdom of the Sea that he stayed on and on, quite forgetting his alphabet.

A long time passed. At last Lamed grew tired of the sea. He wanted to return to the alphabet. But whenever he told Leviathan that he wished to leave the Kingdom of the Sea, the jealous king would order the waves to rock back and forth. The rocking and the rolling of the waves would lull Lamed to sleep and he would forget about returning to his alphabet.

The letters, in the meantime, were very unhappy without their Letter-in-Chief. They stood at the edge of the sea and called and called, "Lamed, Lamed, please come back." But crafty Leviathan made the waters tumble and roar so fiercely that the call of the letters was lost, like a little puff of smoke in the wind.

At last the letters decided that they would get help. They hurried off to Jerusalem and came before Solomon, King of the Jews.

"O Solomon," said the alphabet, "our Letter-in-Chief, Lamed, is visiting Leviathan as his royal guest. He has been there so long that we think he must have forgotten us. Won't you please help us get him back?"

"Indeed, I will," said King Solomon. "Who ever heard of a Hebrew alphabet without a Lamed? Leviathan must be up to some of his tricks."

Solomon rose from his throne and hurried to the shore of the sea. All the letters streamed hopefully behind him.

"Leviathan," called Solomon, "send Lamed up at once."

When Leviathan heard Solomon's voice he was frightened. Then he thought slyly, "I'll pretend that I'm hard of hearing. Solomon can call and call, but it isn't my fault if I can't hear him."

So Leviathan sat back on his throne and pretended he was hard of hearing.

Solomon, standing at the edge of the sea, called again.

"Lamed, come up from the Kingdom of the Sea!"

The voice of King Solomon went straight down through the waters till it reached Lamed. Lamed started to his feet.

"That was the voice of Solomon," he said.

Quickly, Leviathan set the water roaring and tumbling. Louder and louder Solomon called, but his voice was lost in the roar of the waves. Below, in the Kingdom of the Sea, Lamed fell fast asleep, as he always did when the waves roared.

"So," said Solomon to himself, "Leviathan

has set the waves roaring so that Lamed cannot hear me."

Solomon raised his head. Loud and clear his voice rang out over the tumbling sea.

"O waves," he cried, "let your roaring cease. It is I, Solomon, who speaks."

No sooner had Solomon spoken than the towering waves fell back. The sea lay smooth and silent like an endless sheet of glass.

Then Solomon raised his voice and called once more. "Lamed, return to the alphabet!"

Down into the waters went Solomon's voice, deep into the Kingdom of Leviathan. Lamed awoke from his sleep with a start.

"I must return to the alphabet," he said.

Leviathan tried with all his might to set the waves roaring again. But the waters lay still under Solomon's gaze as he stood at the edge of the sea. Lamed rose and left the Kingdom of the Sea while Leviathan sat sullen and helpless on his coral throne.

The letters joyfully welcomed back their

Letter-in-Chief. Never again did Lamed leave his faithful alphabet, not even for a short visit. As for Leviathan, he was so angry that he would not eat for a week.

"Which is punishment enough," said wise King Solomon, "for someone with an appetite as huge as Leviathan's."

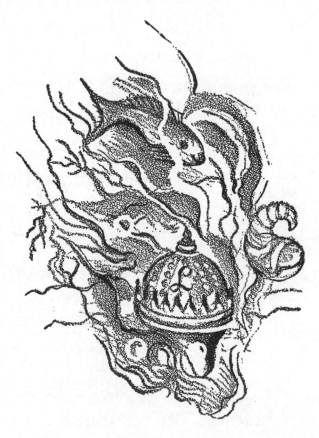

Mem
Mixes Things Up

ONE day the letter Mem decided that he was too plump.

"There's too much of me," said Mem. "I bulge all around. If I bulged just a little more, I would be a ball instead of a letter."

He looked at tall, graceful Letter-in-Chief Lamed. He looked at slender Vav and Zayin and at little Yod. Then Mem made up his mind.

"I am going to reduce," he told the letters of the alphabet.

But the letters were accustomed to Mem just as he was.

"You're all right as you are," they told him.

"I'm too fat," said Mem.

"You're not fat. You're only plump," said Het.

"But **I don't** want to be plump," said Mem.

And away he went to change his shape to a Size One.

Mem began to exercise. First he twisted and turned from side to side. Then he stretched and bent.

Up, down, up, down,
Touch your shoulders, knees and toes,
Up, down, up, down,
Till your feet can touch your nose.

After the twisting and turning and stretching and bending, Mem climbed trees. The taller the trees were, the better Mem liked them, because he had more to climb. Then he tried

running to help him get thin. He ran faster and faster and faster, till his shadow could not catch up with him. After that he squeezed himself into tight places. At first he could hardly get into a tight place. But the more he exercised, the easier it became.

At last Mem was thin. He looked at himself in the clear waters of a spring and saw that he was Size One.

Mem was pleased with himself. He hurried back to the alphabet.

"How do you like me?" he asked.

The letters could hardly believe their eyes.

"But you're not Mem any more," they said. "You're another Vav."

Letter-in-Chief Lamed tried to reason with Mem.

"We can't have a Hebrew alphabet with two Vavs and no Mem," he said.

Mem said he couldn't help it.

The letters coaxed Mem. They said he looked pale and sick. They tried to get him back into shape.

Mem refused.

In the meantime, there was great excitement among the words that had the letter Mem in them.

"We can't have letters just changing any time they want to," one of them said. "Suppose all the letters decide to change."

"There would be nothing left of us," said another word.

"I'm going to talk to Mem about it," said the word Mitzvah.

And Mitzvah went off to see Mem. On the way he met the words Mayim and Mosheh. They were going to see Mem, too. The three words went together.

Mem was admiring his reflection in the water when the three words arrived.

"All the words are very much upset," they told Mem. "They don't need another Vav. They need a Mem."

"I *am* Mem," said Mem.

"You look like Vav," said the word Mayim. "And all the words are going to get mixed up. You're going to spoil a good many stories and books if you don't become plump again."

Mem paid no attention. Instead, he turned his head so that he could see himself better in the water.

"Take me, for instance," said the word Mitzvah. "I mean a good deed. If there is no Mem in the alphabet there won't be a Hebrew word for good deed."

"People can make up another word for good deed," said Mem.

"How about me?" said the word Mayim. "I mean water, so I'm very important. And I have two Mems. If there is no letter Mem

in the alphabet, then there's almost nothing left of me."

"Goodness," said Mem, "people can find another word for water, too."

"Can they find another word for me?" asked the word Mosheh. "Mosheh means Moses, Israel's great teacher. No one can change that name."

Mem was silent. He looked into the water, at his Size One shape. He thought of Moses leading the Jews out of Egypt and giving them the Ten Commandments.

Mem decided that an important name like Moses needed a letter at the beginning that was big and strong. He decided to grow plump again.

"All right," he said to the three words, "I'll stop exercising."

And he did. He stopped bending and turning and twisting. He did not touch his shoulders, knees and toes. He did not run or climb trees or squeeze into tight places.

He just sat.

All the letters stood around and watched him grow. Mem grew bigger and bigger. He grew wider and wider.

At last he was not like Vav any more. He was a very proud letter who was big enough to be the beginning of a great name, Moses.

How the Letters
Helped Nun

MANY years ago, in the land of Babylonia, a baby prince was born. There was great rejoicing in the palace of the king, for now there was an heir to the throne of Babylonia. For seven days and seven nights torches burned in the palace. In the great marble chambers, the noblemen of Babylonia sat on ivory couches toasting the health of the prince.

But when the letters of the Hebrew alphabet heard of the birth of the prince, they were troubled and sad. The letters knew that a Babylonian king would bring war upon the Children of Israel and destroy many homes and vineyards. They wondered if the new-born prince would be that cruel king.

"Let us go to the Babylonian Maker of Names," said Aleph. "Perhaps he will know."

The letters set out for Babylonia. In a cleft of a mountain near the Tigris River, they found the Maker of Names. He was an old man with a white beard that reached to his waist. In his hand he held a chisel tipped with fire. And before him was a huge granite rock on which he was carving the name of the prince.

"Tell us, Maker of Names," said Lamed, "will this prince be the cruel king who will conquer Israel?"

The old man lowered his chisel. He looked toward the hills of Palestine that lay beyond Babylonia. Then he said wearily, "Yes, he will be that king."

The letters of the Hebrew alphabet turned

to the huge granite rock. Already the Babylonian Maker of Names had carved the first letter of the prince's name in the Babylonian language. Under it he was carving the first letter of the name in the Hebrew language.

The Hebrew letters looked at each other. They did not want to be used in the name of a cruel king.

"O Maker of Names," said Lamed, "must this prince have a Hebrew name?"

The old man answered, "Every man must have a name in all the languages of the world."

And he continued to carve the first Hebrew letter of the prince's name.

The letters stood about him and watched the chisel burn its way into the rock. The old man's hand moved slowly. The letters stood silent and anxious.

"I hope it isn't Aleph," thought Aleph.

"Please don't make it Bet," murmured Bet.

"It . . . it looks like Vav," Vav said to himself. "No, it isn't Vav!"

The old man took his chisel from the rock. The first letter was finished. It was the letter Nun.

All the other letters looked at poor Nun. Nun stood very still, gazing at the granite rock. Then he turned to the Maker of Names.

"I don't want to be the first letter of a name that men will hate," he pleaded. "Why must *I* be the first letter?"

"It is too late to change," said the old man. "Nun has already been carved in this granite rock."

"Then let the prince have a name with only one letter," said Zayin.

"No!" Nun cried. "I don't want to be the only letter in his name."

"Of course not," said Zayin quickly. "I didn't think of that."

The Maker of Names lifted his chisel. The fire burned into the rock as he began to carve the second letter of the name.

"Wait!" cried Lamed. "Please wait! Perhaps we can think of some way to help Nun."

"I know!" said Het in great excitement. "Let's all get into the prince's name. Then Nun will have all his friends with him and he won't feel so bad about being the first letter."

"That won't do either," said Nun. "If the name has all the letters it will be too hard for people to pronounce. And if people can't pronounce it, then they will just call him Nun for short. And that's as bad as being the only letter in the name."

The letters agreed with Nun. Once more

the Babylonian Maker of Names put his chisel to the rock.

"Time passes," he said, "and the prince must have his name."

Then Lamed spoke.

"Let as many letters as possible get into this cruel king's name. Not *all* the letters, or people will call him Nun for short. But just enough letters to make Nun feel comfortable, with many friends about him."

The letters nodded at Lamed's wise suggestion.

"So be it," said the Maker of Names.

The old man's white beard stirred in the mountain breeze. He turned and looked thoughtfully for a moment at the palace in the distance where torches flamed into the dark night. Then, with his chisel tipped with fire, he carved the name of the prince into the granite rock.

And that is how it came about that the cruel king of Babylonia had a long and crowded name:

NEBUCHADNEZZAR

Samek
and the Cedar Tree

THE letters of the Hebrew alphabet were deep in sorrow. Nebuchadnezzar, King of Babylonia, had come to Palestine. With his mighty armies, Nebuchadnezzar had conquered Israel. Men and women and children were put into chains. They were led weeping into captivity.

All the land mourned for Israel. The earth gave no wheat or barley or rye. The leaves on the trees turned brown, then died.

Flowers bent their heads to the ground and withered. Even the waters of the Jordan River lashed the shores in sorrow. No bird sang.

The letters of the Hebrew alphabet mourned together with all the land. With the rivers and the seas and the hills and the brown earth, they wept for the Children of Israel.

The letter Samek said, "I shall go to Mount Sinai, for I am the first letter of that great name. Perhaps there I shall find comfort."

Samek went to the Great Desert. He passed the Red Sea, which the Children of Israel had crossed on their way from Egypt to Palestine. The waters of the Red Sea rose and beat against the shore. Through the great desertland the sorrowing voice of the waves was heard:

Weep, beat against the shore,
Israel is seen no more, no more.

Samek went on through the desertland. The hot sirocco winds blew over the endless sands. The trees of the oases shriveled in the heat and the fountains ran dry. No caravans moved over the desert trails for fear of the hot sirocco. For Israel was conquered, and the desert, where Israel had wandered for many years, mourned with all the land.

At last Samek reached Mount Sinai. Heavy black clouds hung over the mount, and deep within it volcanoes rumbled and roared.

"O noble Mount Sinai," wept Samek, "upon your slopes Moses gave the Children of Israel the Ten Commandments. But now you are covered with heavy black clouds. The sun does not shine on your peak. Volcanoes rumble and roar within you. I came to you for comfort. But you mourn for Israel like all the land."

When Samek was silent the voice of Sinai spoke:

"It was here that the Children of Israel

became a nation. Shall I not mourn for them now?"

"Where shall I go for comfort?" asked Samek.

"Go to Mount Nebo, where Moses lies buried," said the voice of Sinai. "There you will find comfort."

Samek went to Nebo that looked out over the Land of Israel. But that mount, too, was shrouded with clouds. The flowers and grass on its slopes were withered. The air was heavy and dark. A desolate wind blew in from the desert. Birds perched with folded wings on the stony crags and were silent.

Samek went up Mount Nebo to its peak,

where Moses lay buried. When he reached the crest, he stopped and looked about him in wonder.

The peak of Mount Nebo lay bright and green under the sky. Through banks of black clouds the sun shone bravely. Everywhere, birds sang and chirped. And from amidst the green grass and leafy trees, like a monarch among them, there rose a stately cedar tree. It lifted its head proudly in the cool, sparkling air, and the rays of the sun made little pools of light and shadow on its soft green leaves.

Samek gazed at the cedar tree and asked, "Why do you rejoice when all the land mourns for Israel?"

The leaves of the cedar tree rustled in the cool breeze. The voice of the cedar was heard, like gentle music over the peak of Mount Nebo.

"Once I was the staff of Moses. He held me in his hand when he went to ask Pharaoh to let his people go. He held me out over the tumbling waters of the Red Sea, and the

sea parted for Israel to pass. He struck me against a rock in the desert when Israel was thirsty for water, and a stream of water gushed forth from the rock. At last, when Moses climbed Mount Nebo, he took me with him. Here Moses died. And I, who had been his staff for many years, became a cedar tree. Like Moses, I do not lose hope. The Children of Israel have been conquered, but they will live forever. Therefore I do not mourn."

The cedar tree was silent. The green leaves danced in the summer breeze. The sun shone brightly on the mountain peak where Moses lay buried.

And Samek was comforted at last. For he knew that Israel, like the staff of Moses, would live forever.

The Mystery
of the
Letter Ayin

THE letter Ayin was very proud of his name. That was because his name meant eye.

"What is more important than an eye?" asked Ayin. "It opens and it shuts. It can see far away and it can see very near. And best of all, it can read."

And because his name meant eye, the letter Ayin was the best reader in the alphabet. He read anything that had words —

geography, history, stories. Ayin liked stories best of all, especially adventure stories.

Now the letter Ayin did not have any books of his own to read. Whenever he wanted to read a story he went to a place that had books. Sometimes he went to a library. Sometimes he went to the house of a scribe. He was the man who wrote books. And sometimes he went to the house of a scholar. He was the man who bought books. When Ayin finished reading his story he would return to the alphabet and tell the letters what he had read.

One day Ayin wanted to read a story. This time he went to the house of a scholar. The scholar was not at home when Ayin called. He was in school, teaching children how to read.

Ayin went into the room where the scholar kept his books. He soon found a story book. One of the stories was about a poor shepherd whose name was Akiba. Ayin liked the story at once because Akiba's name began with the letter Ayin.

He began to read. First he read page one. When he finished page one he read page two. Then he turned to page three. He was in the middle of page three when the scholar came home from school.

Now it happened that the scholar also wanted to read the story about Akiba. He began on page one, just as Ayin had done. Then he read page two. After that he went to page three. He was a faster reader than Ayin because he was a wise scholar. So when he got to page four he caught up with the letter Ayin.

The scholar stared and stared at Ayin. He could hardly believe his eyes.

"Goodness," he said, "I have read this story many times and I never found an extra Ayin on this page. This Ayin doesn't belong in the story at all!"

The scholar closed his eyes and opened

them again. Ayin was still there, on page four.

"Perhaps," said the scholar, "there is something the matter with my spectacles."

He hurried out of his house and went to the store to buy a new pair of spectacles. In the meantime, the letter Ayin finished pages four and five. He was on page six when the scholar returned.

The scholar looked at page four through his new spectacles. Ayin was not there. He was on page six.

The scholar read page four and page five and page six. When he got to page seven, there was Ayin again.

"There is that Ayin again!" cried the scholar. "First he was on page four and now he's on page seven. There is nothing the matter with my spectacles, because I just bought new ones. Perhaps there is something the matter with my eyes."

The scholar took a nap to rest his eyes. And while he napped, Ayin read page seven and eight and nine. Then the scholar woke up and went back to his story. When he got to page ten he found Ayin again.

"There is nothing the matter with my spectacles and there is nothing the matter with my eyes," he said. "And whoever heard of an Ayin that appears first on one page and then on another? I simply can't understand it."

And he rushed off to his friend who lived next door. His friend was a wise scholar, too. The first scholar told the second about the mysterious Ayin. Then the two scholars came to have a look at the story of Akiba.

They read pages one, two, three, four, five, six, seven, eight, nine, ten, eleven, twelve, thirteen. On page fourteen they found Ayin. He was a fast reader.

The first scholar looked at the second scholar and the second looked at the first. They were so astonished they could not say a word. Then they ran out to call more scholars.

They went to all the scholars in the city. They went wherever scholars are to be found — in libraries and in schools and in museums. And they told them about the mysterious Ayin.

The scholars took their fat books. They took their Encyclopedias and Dictionaries and Grammars and Books of Rules. And they came running.

They put on their spectacles and they began to search for the mysterious Ayin. They began on page one and they searched every page till they reached page seventeen. And there, on page seventeen, they found him.

The scholars stared at Ayin. They looked at each other and back at Ayin. They scratched their heads. They puckered their brows. Then they looked in their fat books for rules about an extra Ayin in the Akiba story. They looked in the Encyclopedias and in the Dictionaries and in the Grammars and in the Books of Rules. But they could not

find any rule about an extra Ayin in the Akiba story.

The scholars decided to go to the rabbi, who was the wisest man in the city. They found him reading his Bible, and told him about the mysterious Ayin. The rabbi closed his Bible. He put on his long black coat and his round black hat. And he went to the first scholar's house with all the scholars of the city behind him.

When they got there they began to read the Akiba story. They read from page one to page eighteen. Page eighteen was the last page of the story. And Ayin wasn't anywhere to be found. That was because he had finished the story and had gone home.

"There is no extra Ayin anywhere," said the rabbi.

"But we saw him," said the scholars. "He was on page seventeen."

"It must have been your imagination," said the rabbi.

And he went home to his Bible.

As for the scholars, they just sat there and stared at each other through their round spectacles. And to the end of their days they talked about the mysterious Ayin who vanished in thin air as soon as the rabbi came to have a look at him.

Peh and His Friend
the Shofar

Do RE me, me re do,
Up and down the scale I go,
Singing fa sol la te do
When the cock begins to crow.

This was the letter Peh's morning song.
For Peh, whose name means mouth, loved
to sing and talk and make up poems and
jingles. But most of all, Peh loved to imitate
his friends. And Peh had many friends —
bells, trumpets, horns, anvils, echoes, footsteps — all kinds of things that made sounds.
Every day Peh visited his friends and practiced the sounds they made.

One of Peh's best friends was a shofar, which is a trumpet made of a ram's horn. This shofar lived in a synagogue, and he could make some of the loudest sounds Peh had ever heard. When the rabbi put the shofar to his lips and blew, the voice of the shofar would ring out so bravely that the walls of the synagogue shook.

This shofar was blown on very important holidays, when the synagogue was full of people. Whenever one of these holidays came round, Peh visited the synagogue to hear his friend shake the walls with his beautiful shofar-voice.

One day Peh went to visit his friend the shofar. To his surprise, Peh found him looking troubled.

"Why, what's the matter?" asked Peh.

The shofar shook his head sadly and did not answer.

"Have you lost your voice?" asked Peh.

"It's almost as bad as that," said the shofar in a funny squeak. "I have a sore throat. And tomorrow is an important holi-day. I don't know what to do."

"Do you mean you won't be able to use your voice?" asked Peh anxiously.

"How can I, with a cold?" said the shofar. "The rabbi thinks it's his fault. He thinks he has forgotten how to blow me. Here he comes now," the shofar added gloomily.

At that moment the rabbi came walking down the empty synagogue. He picked up the shofar from the table and put it to his lips. He blew. A tiny squeak that sounded like a mouse came out.

"Oh dear," said the rabbi, "why can't I blow the shofar? I'll try again."

And he put it to his lips and blew with all his might. An-other squeak came out. The rabbi blew and blew. He huffed and he puffed. His face grew red. He turned the shofar this way and that. At last he gave up.

"I hope I'll be able to blow the shofar tomorrow," he said gravely.

And he left the synagogue and went home.

"The rabbi doesn't know about my sore throat," the shofar told Peh. "Poor man."

"Maybe your throat will feel better tomorrow," Peh comforted his friend.

The shofar sighed.

"I'm afraid it won't," he said. "It feels very raw."

Peh suddenly had an idea. He got so excited that he almost fell off the table.

"I'll take your place tomorrow," he told his friend.

"Please stop talking riddles," said the shofar. "How can you take my place?"

"It's easy," Peh went on. "I can make the same sounds you make, with a little more practice."

"You mean—" began the shofar hopefully.

Peh danced up and down.

"I mean I'll hide in you," he explained

eagerly. "And when the rabbi blows, I'll imitate your beautiful loud voice. And no one will know."

This time it was the shofar who got excited. He said he would be grateful all his life. And he begged Peh to come on time the next day, or the rabbi and all the people in the synagogue would be disappointed.

Peh hurried away. He went to a forest to spend the night because he did not want to disturb the alphabet with his practicing.

All the forest animals came to listen as Peh's voice rang through the trees like a loud, clear shofar-blast. The lion thought Peh ought to get a bit of roaring into his voice, and the bear thought a growl would sound better.

Peh practiced all night. The next day he rushed back to the synagogue. The shofar was so glad to see him he almost lost whatever voice he still had.

"I'm glad you came," he whispered to Peh. "Just look at all the people. And look at the rabbi. He looks terribly worried."

"Now don't you worry," said Peh.

And he crept into the shofar and waited.

An hour passed. It was so quiet in the shofar Peh almost fell asleep. Two hours passed. Peh dozed off because he had been awake all night practicing, and he was a bit sleepy. Three hours passed. Peh was fast asleep.

The rabbi picked up the shofar. A worried line creased his forehead as he put the shofar to his lips. The rabbi blew. Not a sound came.

All the people in the synagogue leaned forward anxiously.

"Wake up!" the shofar whispered to Peh. "Please wake up!"

Peh awoke with a start. The rabbi put the shofar to his lips again.

"Ready?" whispered the shofar.

"Ready," whispered Peh.

The rabbi blew. Out came the voice of Peh in a loud and beautiful shofar-blast. The rabbi smiled happily. Again he put the shofar to his lips and blew. Loud and clear came

Peh's shofar-voice, making the walls of the synagogue tremble and shake. Again and again the rabbi blew. Up and down, up and down went Peh's voice. Bold and clear the call of the shofar rang forth, till the vast synagogue was filled with brave, echoing sounds.

And when it was all over and everyone had gone home, the shofar sighed happily.

"Why, you sounded so much like me I couldn't tell the difference myself," he said to Peh.

"Oh, that," said Peh modestly. "There's no sound a mouth can't make, with a little practice."

And a very satisfied Peh went home to tell the alphabet about his adventure in the shofar.

Why the Letter Tzade Follows the Letter Peh

TZADE was a very gentle, modest letter. He was the beginning of many gentle, modest words:

> Tzvi — deer
> Tzadik — righteous
> Tzippor — bird
> Tzon — sheep
> Tzanuah — modest

Tzade was not only gentle and modest. He was very bashful. He never volunteered to be in a word. The other letters had to urge him. And Tzade was a quiet letter. He liked to sit by himself and think.

Now it happened, in the early days of the alphabet, that the letters were getting into alphabetical order. They were all busy choosing their places. They decided that Aleph would be first and Bet would be second. Gimel said he wanted to be third and Dalet wanted to stand near Gimel.

Tzade did not seem to want anything. He just wanted to be quiet and gentle.

"What about you, Tzade?" asked Lamed. "Where do you want to stand?"

"Oh, me," said Tzade. "Don't bother about me."

"But you must have a place in the alphabet," Lamed said.

Tzade thought for a moment, then he said, "If you don't mind, I'd like to be last."

"Being last is very important," said Lamed. "The last letter brings up the rear, and that's important."

"Well then," said Tzade, "I'll just tag along behind the rear."

The letters did not want Tzade tagging along behind the rear. They thought he ought to have a regular place in the alphabet, like everyone else. So they put him next to Peh. They hoped that being next to Peh, who was always singing and jingling and making sounds, would make Tzade feel a little bolder.

So Tzade took his place next to Peh. But he was very uncomfortable. Peh was never quiet for a moment. Just as Tzade would get ready to think quietly, Peh would growl like a bear or roar like a lion.

"I don't like to complain," thought timid Tzade, "but I do wish Peh were a little quieter."

Even at night Tzade hardly got a wink of sleep. As soon as night came, there was Peh hooting like an owl. The next night he was imitating a rushing river. And the next night he was a company of soldiers marching across a wooden bridge to meet the enemy. Tzade got so that he jumped at the slightest sound.

One day the letters went off to make up some new words. Peh, who was in a very cheerful mood, was imitating a field of crickets. Tzade could not stand the noise. After a while he stepped away from Peh and tagged along behind the rear, at the very end of the alphabet.

Louder and louder sounded the crickets. Tzade walked very slowly, till there was a space between him and the alphabet. Peh suddenly imitated his friend the shofar. Tzade was so startled he jumped into the air, then he sat down on a stone to rest.

The alphabet went on, never missing Tzade. When Peh's voice died away in the distance Tzade got up to follow his friends. After he had walked for a while he noticed that he had taken the wrong path. The alphabet was nowhere in sight.

Tzade ran back and took another path.

Then another and another. At last poor, frightened Tzade did not know where to turn. He was lost and very lonely.

"If only I could hear Peh's jolly voice," sighed Tzade.

But the alphabet was so far away that even Peh's loudest shouts could not reach him.

Tzade wandered here and he wandered there. He walked up mountain sides and down valleys. At last he was so tired that he just lay down and fell asleep.

When Tzade awoke he found that he was in a strange place. Many odd little creatures were standing about him, watching him curiously. Tzade sat gazing at them, wondering why they looked so familiar. Then he recognized them. They were the letters of an old, old alphabet that nobody was using any more.

"How do you do," said Tzade politely.

The old letters began to make queer sounds.

"Dear me," thought Tzade, "what are they saying?" And aloud he said, "I'm lost. Can you tell me how to find my way back to the Hebrew alphabet?"

The old letters made more sounds. They asked Tzade if there was anything he wanted. But Tzade could not understand a word. They asked how the Hebrew alphabet was getting along. They talked louder and louder, hoping Tzade would understand them. Tzade had never heard so many strange sounds.

"*Now* look at me," he sighed, "lost in a foreign language."

The letters were very kind to Tzade. They tried to make him comfortable. They told him stories about themselves. Tzade got tired of hearing all their strange sounds. He missed his friends in the Hebrew alphabet, especially jolly Peh, who was always making familiar sounds. Tzade felt miserable.

Suddenly he heard a voice in the distance. It was a familiar voice this time. It came from far away and it seemed to say, "Tzade, Tzade, where are you?"

Tzade jumped up.

"That sounds like my dear friend Peh," he thought happily. "Or is it only my imagination?"

"Tzade, Tzade," came the voice again.

"Can it really be Peh?" said Tzade hopefully. "Oh, dear."

There were a few moments of silence. Tzade walked anxiously back and forth, gazing in every direction. Then he jumped high into the air as he heard the roar of a lion and the growl of a bear. Then came the call of the shofar and the thunder of waves on a stormy night. All the letters of the foreign alphabet ran behind trees to hide.

"It *is* Peh!" cried Tzade. "It's my good friend Peh!"

In a little while, to Tzade's delight, Peh came running up to him. For when the Hebrew letters had found that Tzade was lost, they sent Peh, who could make the loudest noise, to look for him.

Tzade said good-by to the foreign alphabet. Of course, the letters could not understand him, but they were sorry to see him go. They stood shouting farewell till Peh and Tzade were out of sight.

After that, Tzade never stirred from Peh's side. He grew to love Peh's noises and sounds. Sometimes, when no one was listening, he even tried to imitate them. But most of the time he was happy to just listen.

And that is why Tzade always follows Peh in the Hebrew alphabet.

Kof and the Woodcutter's Prayer

THE letter Kof stands at the beginning of the word Kadosh. Kadosh means holy, and it was Kof's favorite word. He liked all kinds of holy things. His best friends were synagogues, Bibles, praying-shawls, Holy Arks, prayers.

One day Kof was walking through the forest. It was Friday evening, and he was on his way home from the synagogue where he had been listening to the Sabbath prayers.

Suddenly Kof heard a gentle stir among

the trees. Kof stopped. "What can it be?" he thought. Through the shadows something was coming toward him. Kof gazed in wonder. It was a little prayer. Kof had never met a prayer in the forest before. He saw at once that it was a beautiful prayer.

"Good Sabbath," said the prayer sadly.

"Good Sabbath," said Kof. "I have never seen you before. Who are you?"

"I am a Sabbath prayer," was the answer. "I belong to a woodcutter who lives in the forest."

"Why are you so sad?" asked Kof.

"Because my woodcutter is ashamed of me," said the little Sabbath prayer.

"Why is he ashamed of you?" asked Kof in surprise. "You are very beautiful, as beautiful as any of the prayers in the synagogue."

"My woodcutter is a poor man," the little prayer explained, "and a very kind one. He lives so far from the synagogue that he cannot go there to pray. And he is unhappy because he cannot read the prayer book. So he made me up as his special Sabbath prayer. But he thinks I am not as good as the prayers they recite in the synagogue."

Kof felt sorry for the little prayer.

"All prayers are good," said Kof, "if the person who recites them is good."

"My woodcutter does not know that," sighed the prayer, "though he is a very good man."

Kof wished he could help the little prayer. He decided to come back the next week to see how it was getting along.

The following Friday, late in the afternoon, Kof passed through the forest again on his way to the synagogue.

"I will stop at the woodcutter's house on my way back," thought Kof. "Perhaps I will meet the little prayer then."

Kof had not gone far before he saw a rabbi walking along the forest trail. The rabbi kept looking at the darkening sky.

"It is getting late," he said. "The Sabbath will arrive before I can get out of the forest. I must spend the Sabbath here."

The rabbi looked around and saw the woodcutter's house.

"I will ask the woodcutter if I may spend the Sabbath with him," he said.

Kof followed the rabbi to the woodcutter's house. He saw him knock on the door. Soon there were footsteps and the woodcutter appeared. He gazed at his visitor in great surprise.

"Good evening, rabbi," he said.

"Good evening, good woodcutter," said the rabbi. "I was walking through the forest when I saw your house. The Sabbath is almost here, and it is too late to travel farther. May I spend the Sabbath with you?"

"You are welcome to my humble house," said the poor woodcutter.

And he opened the door wide for his Sabbath guest.

Kof followed the rabbi into the house. He stood quietly in a corner to see what would happen.

Everything in the house was bright and clean. Sabbath candles stood on the table. The tablecloth was as white as snow. The dishes sparkled. There were gay flowers on the window-sill. The woodcutter and his wife and children were neatly dressed in their Sabbath clothes.

The woodcutter's wife lit the candles and recited a blessing.

"Amen," said the woodcutter and his children.

"Amen," said the rabbi.

"Amen," said Kof.

The rabbi began to recite his prayers. The woodcutter turned his face away and was silent.

"Why are you silent?" the rabbi asked.

"I am an ignorant man," answered the woodcutter. "I cannot read the prayers in the prayer book, so I made up my own Sabbath prayer. But it is not good enough to recite together with your prayers, good rabbi."

"Let me hear your Sabbath prayer," the rabbi said kindly.

The woodcutter hesitated for a moment, then he recited:

> I thank You, O Lord, for all
> You have given me, for my
> dear wife and children who give
> me joy and comfort, for the

roof over my head to protect
me, for the bread I eat that
gives strength to my arms,
and for the love that fills my
heart when I think of You and
Your kindness. Amen.

"Amen," said the rabbi softly.

"Amen," murmured Kof.

The little prayer came and stood beside
Kof.

"You see," it said sadly, "my woodcutter
is ashamed of me."

"Just listen to what the rabbi is telling
your woodcutter," said Kof.

The little prayer listened eagerly.

The rabbi was speaking to the woodcutter
with a gentle smile. "That is one of the most
beautiful prayers I have ever heard," he
said.

"No, rabbi," began the woodcutter. "I
am only an ignorant man —"

"Beautiful prayers come from a kind

heart," said the rabbi. "And because your heart is kind, your prayer is beautiful."

The woodcutter's eyes filled with tears.

"Thank you, rabbi," he said.

The rabbi began to recite his own prayers. The little Sabbath prayer turned to Kof and said happily, "The rabbi says I am a beautiful prayer."

"And your woodcutter will not be ashamed of you any more," said Kof.

The little prayer looked at the wood-cutter. His face was as bright and shining as the candles that filled the house with their Sabbath light.

The Wisdom
of the
Letter Resh

THE letter Resh, whose name means head, was very wise. All the other letters used to come to Resh with their problems, which he always solved. Even Lamed, Letter-in-Chief of the alphabet, often asked Resh for advice about alphabet affairs.

But the letters did not know how very wise Resh was until . . . .

One day a Beautiful Story came to the alphabet. The Beautiful Story was troubled and needed some sensible advice.

"I've come to see you," said the Beautiful Story, "because I'm in terrible danger."

"What kind of danger?" Lamed asked.

"I'm in danger of being forgotten," said the Beautiful Story.

The letters gathered about and the Beautiful Story continued.

"For many years I have been living in a certain family. A father would tell me to his son, and when the son became a father he would tell me to his son. And so I passed from father to son for many generations. But now, the only father who knows me has no son. His son died, and he has no one to tell me to. And I'm afraid I shall be forgotten."

"That would be a pity," said Ayin, who loved stories.

"Where does this father live?" asked Resh.

"He lives in a little white house in the village," said the Beautiful Story. "And he is very lonely."

The letters were silent as they all sat thinking. They thought and thought. Then Resh said, "If this father had a son you would not be forgotten."

The Beautiful Story nodded.

"Then what we must do," declared Resh, "is find a son for this father."

All the letters agreed. They ran off to find a son. Resh and the Beautiful Story remained behind.

In a little while the letters returned.

"We found a son," said Gimel. "He has black hair and brown eyes and he's just right."

"Where did you find him?" asked Resh.

"In a red house, where he is living with his father," said Dalet.

"That's the wrong kind of son," said Resh. "You must find a son without a father."

The letters went off again. They stayed away longer this time. But after a while they returned.

"We found a son without a father," Vav told Resh. "He has brown hair and blue eyes and he lives with his mother and —"

"No," Resh interrupted. "The son we need should have neither a father nor a mother. He must be an orphan. And never mind the color of his hair and eyes. It doesn't matter."

Away went the letters again, to find an orphan. They were gone for a long time. The Beautiful Story was becoming more and more impatient, when at last they returned with good news.

"We found a son without a father or a mother," said the letters happily. "He lives all alone in a little house in the forest."

"Good," said Resh. "Now we have a son who needs a father." Then he turned to the Beautiful Story and asked, "Does anyone live with the father who needs a son?"

"No," said the Beautiful Story, "only a cow who lives in the barn."

Resh thought for several moments. The letters waited. Then Resh said, "We must get the cow to the forest."

"But how do we get the cow to the forest?" asked the letters.

Resh thought some more. Then he said to Peh, "Run over to the barn where the cow lives and ask her to please go to the forest and get lost."

Peh did as he was told. He went to the barn and asked the cow to go to the forest and get lost. The cow said, "All right, if it's just for a little while." And she left the barn and went off to the forest, while Peh returned to the alphabet.

"What do we do next?" the letters asked Resh.

"Nothing," said Resh. "Now see what happens."

The letters and the Beautiful Story watched eagerly. They saw the father who needed a son go to the barn to fetch his cow. But the barn was empty, for the cow was in the forest. The man looked everywhere for his cow. He called and called. But there was no answer. The man was lonelier than ever, for now he did not even have a cow.

Now, the son who needed a father came out of his little house. He was lonely, too, for he did not even have a cow, either. Suddenly he heard a loud moo, and there, under an oak tree, he found the cow.

"What a lovely cow," said the son. "She would be a good companion, if only she were mine. But I must return her to her master."

And he led the cow out of the forest to the little white house in the village where the father who needed a son lived.

The man was sitting in front of his house, feeling lonely. Along came the son who needed a father, leading the cow.

"Here is your cow," he said. "I found her in the forest."

"Oh, thank you," said the man. "I'm very lonely without my cow." Then he asked, "Where do you live?"

"I live all alone in a house in the forest," said the son who needed a father.

"Don't you have a father?" asked the man.

"No," said the son, "but I would like to have one."

"And I would like to have a son,"

said the man. "Won't you please come and live with me?"

"Thank you," said the son, "I will."

And he moved into the man's house at once.

Very soon after, the father began to tell stories to his new son. And the very first story he told him was the Beautiful Story that had come to the alphabet for help.

So the Beautiful Story was not forgotten. And all because of Resh, who was the wisest of all the letters.

Shin's Daydream

THE letter Shin was a dreamer. He was the first letter of the word Shabbat, which means Sabbath, so he liked to stay at home and rest. While he rested, he would daydream. This is one of Shin's daydreams.

One day Shin was walking along a winding road. The road led through open fields. Above him the sun shone and the birds sang. Shin sang with them.

Shin reached a turn in the road. Under a tree beside the road he saw an old, broken candlestick. Shin stopped to talk to the candlestick.

"Why are you lying beside the road," he asked, "and why are you twisted and broken?"

"I belonged to a kind old woman," said the candlestick. "She was very fond of me. I am only made of copper, but every Friday morning she polished me till I shone like gold. When the Sabbath came, I stood proudly on the table, and the candle within me filled the house with bright Sabbath light. And then —"

The candlestick paused for a moment in its tale. Then it went on sadly, "One night thieves broke into the house. They stole me, for they thought I was made of gold. But when they found that I was only copper, they threw me away. And here I lie, twisted and broken, though once I was bright and beautiful enough to welcome the Sabbath."

Shin pitied the candlestick, but there was nothing he could do to help it. He continued on his way.

He followed the winding road through fields and meadows. Near a large stone in the middle of a green meadow he came upon a praying-shawl. It was torn and soiled. Shin stopped to talk to the praying-shawl.

"Why are you lying in the meadow," he asked, "and why are you torn and soiled?"

"Once I belonged to a man," said the praying-shawl. "He was a good, pious man. Every Sabbath, before he prayed, he put me on his shoulders. One day the man found a precious jewel. He sold the jewel and became rich. From that moment, he stopped being good and pious. He became greedy and cruel, instead. He did not pray any more. One day he opened a chest and found me lying there. 'I don't want this old praying-shawl any more,' he said. And he threw me out-of-doors. A wind picked me up and blew me to this meadow."

Shin pitied the praying-shawl, but there was nothing he could do to help it. He continued on his way.

He walked through the meadow and crossed a rippling stream. Beyond the stream was an old, broken-down house. Near one of the walls, a Bible lay on the ground. It was torn and spattered with mud. Shin stopped to talk to the Bible.

"Why are you lying on the ground," asked Shin, "and why are you spattered with mud?"

The Bible told Shin its story.

"A happy family once lived in this house, a father, a mother and three sons. I was their most treasured possession. Every Sabbath the father read me to his wife and his three sons. They spent many hours talking about my beautiful stories and poems.

Then the father and mother grew old and died. The sons went to live in another land, for they were no longer happy here. But they forgot to take me with them. Now a storm has blown down the house. And here I lie, alone and forgotten."

Shin pitied the Bible, but there was nothing he could do to help it. He continued on his way.

Soon he came to a hill. He climbed the hill till he reached the top. When he got there, it was already evening. The air was cool and the sky was growing dark. A white cloud hung over the hilltop, and upon it Shin saw the Sabbath Queen. She was dressed in soft, glowing white, and her eyes were filled with tears.

"Beautiful Sabbath Queen," said Shin, "why do you sit weeping on a cloud?"

"I weep because I am filled with sorrow," said the Sabbath Queen.

"Why are you filled with sorrow?" asked Shin.

The Sabbath Queen answered, "I grieve for the broken candlestick, the torn praying-shawl and the old Bible. These three once helped make the Sabbath beautiful. Now they lie neglected and forgotten."

"But the people are waiting for you on earth," said Shin.

"How can I descend to earth grieving," said the Sabbath Queen, "and bring sorrow with me?"

"Can nothing change your grief to joy?" asked Shin.

"Only you can help," said the Sabbath Queen. "You are the first letter of Shabbat. Through your touch, the candlestick, the praying-shawl and the Bible can bring joy to the Sabbath again."

Shin descended the hillside. He made his way back to the Bible and the praying-shawl and the candlestick. Gently, he touched them. And with his touch, each changed into a star which flew up to the crown of the Sabbath Queen. There they shone with a bright, silvery light.

Shin watched the Sabbath Queen come down to earth. Her face glowed with happiness. Tenderly, the people welcomed her. And she moved among them, spreading Sabbath peace and joy.

Shin's happy daydream was over. He had helped bring the Sabbath Queen to earth.

Tav

Closes the Book

TAV WAS the last letter in the Hebrew alphabet and it was time for his story. But Tav did not have a story.

"Why didn't you get yourself a story?" asked Lamed. "You had plenty of time."

"I'm sorry," said Tav, "but I was busy."

"We were all busy," Lamed told him.

"Not as busy as I was," explained Tav. "I'm the first letter of Torah, and I was busy studying the Torah. And the Torah is big, you know."

The letters were annoyed.

"Now what are we going to do?" they asked. "We can't close the book because you were too busy to get yourself a story."

"I'll tell you one of the stories in the Torah," Tav offered. "How about Adam?"

"No," objected Aleph, Bet, Gimel, Dalet and Hey. "He's in our stories."

"Then I'll tell you a story about the Torah," said Tav. "Will that do?"

"That will do," said Lamed.

And Tav told his story.

Once upon a time there lived a rich man. This man had three sons.

One day the man called his sons and said to them, "I am growing old. When the time comes for me to die, I want to leave most of my wealth to the wisest of you. Go forth into the world. Each of you take a different path. In a year and a day you must return, bringing what you think is the most precious thing in the world. Then I shall know which of you is the wisest and he shall inherit my wealth."

The sons mounted their horses and went forth into the world. Together they followed a highway that led out of the city into the forest. In the middle of the forest the highway divided into three paths. The three brothers promised to meet at the same place in a year and a day. Then each took a different path and rode off.

Spring passed slowly. Summer came, and the leaves turned a deep green. In the autumn the leaves fell softly to the ground. Winter's snow covered the trees like a white blanket and icy winds blew in from the north. Then the warm spring came and the snow melted. Green buds opened into leaves again and tender shoots pushed their way above the brown earth.

At last the three brothers came riding down the forest paths to the meeting of the

roads. Each brother carried in a strong box the treasure he had found to be the most precious in the world.

The brothers embraced and rode on together to their father's house. That night, after the evening meal, they laid their boxes at their father's feet.

The first son spoke.

"I traveled for many days," he said, "through strange and faraway lands. Wherever I went I sought the most precious thing in the world.

"One day I was riding along a dark lane. Suddenly I heard a cry for help. I put spurs to my horse and galloped to the place from where the cry had come. In a glade among the trees I found a man beset by three thieves. Jumping from my horse, I fell upon the thieves and drove them away. The man thanked me many times for saving his life. 'Come to my home with me,' he said, 'and I will reward you.' And he led me to a great mansion that stood on a green hill.

"The man led me into his treasure chamber. I looked about me. There were rare pictures on the walls and rich tapestries that hung from ceiling to floor. On small ebony tables stood costly vases and urns from distant lands. Caskets overflowing with gold and jewels stood against the walls of the room.

" 'Take anything you wish,' the man said. 'Whatever is in my home, is yours.' "

The first son opened the box he had brought. Within it lay a gold wrought casket. As he lifted the lid the room was suddenly lit with the sparkle of a heap of precious jewels.

"This casket of jewels," said the first son, "I chose as the most precious thing in the world."

The father looked at the casket of jewels, nodded his head, and turned to the second son.

"And what have you brought, my son?" he asked.

"When I left my brothers," said the second son, "I rode on for seven days and seven nights till I reached the Great Sea. I boarded a vessel sailing to the land of the mighty King Selim. When I reached the land of King Selim he was at war with a neighboring kingdom.

"I joined Selim's army, where I performed many heroic deeds. Soon the king heard of my bravery and he appointed me commander of many fighting men. When the war was over, the king invited me to live in his palace as one of his courtiers. The days passed like beautiful dreams.

"At last the time came for me to return home. I went to King Selim and told him that I must leave his kingdom. The king was sorry to see me go.

" 'You have served me well,' he said, 'but I cannot keep you here. Before you go, choose something to take with you. Whatever is in my palace is yours.' "

The second son opened the box he had

brought. Within it lay a glittering sword of fine steel. Encrusted on its hilt were red rubies, and each ruby was like a warm drop of blood.

"This is what I chose as the most precious thing in the world," said the second son, "the mighty sword of King Selim the Conqueror."

The father looked at the sword, nodded his head, then turned to the third son.

"And you, my son," he said, "what have you brought?"

The third son began his story.

"On the third day after I left my brothers I came to a small village. There I found a school where young men from every land came to study the Torah. I became a student, too, and I spent my days and nights studying. Often I did not have food enough to eat and my eyes grew weary with poring over the printed words. But I did not leave the school, for it was only in the study of the Torah that I was happy.

"The year passed quickly. When the time came for me to leave I went to my teacher, who was a wise old scholar, and told him that I must return home.

" 'Take what pleases you most,' he said, 'something you will treasure for the rest of your days.' "

The third son opened his box. Within it lay an old Scroll of the Torah.

"I have found the Torah to be the most precious thing in the world," he said.

The father looked at the casket of precious gems, at the sword of fine steel, and at the old Torah. Then he said to the first son, "You have brought back wealth as the most precious thing in the world." And to the second son he said, "And you have brought back power." Then he turned to the third son. "And you, the youngest of my sons, have brought back wisdom."

The father rose and approached the youngest of the brothers.

"You are the wisest of my sons," he went

on, "and you shall inherit my wealth. For you have learned that wisdom is the most precious thing on earth."

Tav ended his story.

"Is it all right?" he asked anxiously.

"It's a good story," said the letters. "Now you can close the book."

And with this story about the three sons Tav closed the book.